The Merchant
of Noises

THE MERCHANT OF NOISES

by Anna Rozen, illustrated by François Avril

translated from the French by Carl W. Scarbrough

DAVID R. GODINE · Publisher · Boston

His name was Mister Bing. A name with its future written upon it, like Doctor Pill or Mister Bread, the baker. One day, as he was walking through the forest, a twig broke loose from a tree and fell on a dried-out tree stump.

Klackata!

"What a lovely sound, that Klackata," thought Mister Bing. Quick as a wink, he collected the branch and dug up the stump. He was quite delighted by that Klackata and — though he was a modest fellow — he thought, "If I enjoyed that Klackata, it just might please someone else. Tomorrow I'll take it to the market and sell it."

The next day, he set himself up between the sock merchant and the sausage seller, and started his sales pitch: "Klackata! Come and hear my wonderful Klackata!"

A cautious-looking gentleman approached the stand, tried out the Klackata, and pulled a disgusted face, declaring, "It's nothing . . . useless!"

Mister Bing had no time to be upset; a woman looking for a present for her little boy happily bought him the Klackata, without even asking the price.

On his way home he passed through the woods once more. He was listening idly to the last drops of a rain shower trickling through the tall trees when he was struck by the sound of the very last droplet of rain as it landed on a leaf — a sort of TRIKA he found especially harmonious. Just to be sure he didn't forget it, Mister Bing hummed all the way home:

"TRIKA, TRIKA, TRIKA, TROK!"

The moment he got home, without even stopping for dinner, he dashed to his work-shop and set to work.

Mister Bing didn't sleep a wink, but he was sure he'd done a good night's work. The TRIKA worked like a charm. And he'd begun tinkering with a marvelous FOOOBOOLOOOOOOO FWEEEEEEEEE. It was an elegant and thoroughly up-to-date item, inspired by the song of his teakettle, though it needed to be perfected before it could be offered to the public. With that, he made the daring decision to speed up production. He took on kindly Mister Patrick as his right-hand man, whose first assignment was to make an enormous billboard.

The gamble paid off; over the next weeks, Mr. Bing had no trouble selling his new marvels. He even dreamed of expanding his little workshop. Inventions followed at an astonishing rate. Mister Bing was happier and happier.

Still, one thing troubled him; he couldn't lay his hands on the proto-type for a rather nice *TrooLOOOOlooo* that he'd just about finished. He'd searched every nook and cranny of his workshop, the closets of his cottage, the very wrinkles of his poor head. . . . The thing had utterly disappeared.

Months passed and as Mr. Bing's success grew, and he had to face facts: he couldn't go it alone any longer. Between a *ZwimmmmZooom* (of which he was really rather proud) and a Tweetifleet (that still gave him pause) there was too much for any one person to do. All the more since the matter of the missing *Troo-LOOOOlooo* never ceased to trouble him.

So he took on a secretary, Mrs. Shorthand, a serious but pleasant young woman who, he hoped, could bring a little order to his business and — who knows? — might even bring a little harmony to his household.

One day, as he worked like a demon on the development of a soon-to-be-famous *Splooooshhhhhooushhhh*, angry cries rang out behind the door. "Let me in! I have a few choice words for that crook . . . that thief . . . that. . . ."

A furious man burst in, red as a beet. Hardly through the door, he waved a limp, disjointed object at Mister Bing's face crying, "Take back your lousy *SkoOOBOOoom*, you cheap fraud!"

Now if there was one thing over which Mister Bing did not quibble, it was quality. This pitiful *SkoOOBOOoom* surely hadn't come from his shop. He would have liked to send the fellow packing, but that would hardly have been good for business. So he calmly invited his visitor to look over the latest models. An hour later, the angry man left, relaxed as a steamed zucchini, with a broad smile and an amusing pocket-model noise from Bing.

The following night, Mister Bing couldn't sleep a wink.
One idea tormented him horribly: someone, somewhere,
was making shoddy, cut-rate noises, but all
the complaints were coming back to him.
He'd managed to calm one unhappy
customer, but there would be more.
And if word got around,
there would be
all sorts of noise.

Hoping to calm himself, he tried to draw. He sketched ultra-perfect mechanisms meant to produce the most refined sounds when — all of a sudden — a terrible CREEEEeeeeeeK made him jump.

It must have come from the workshop. Intrigued, he crept downstairs, armed only with a *ZWIPPP* that wasn't quite finished.

He trembled a bit. A bothersome 𝕂𝕝𝕒𝕜𝕒𝕥𝕒-𝕂𝕝𝕒𝕜 accompanied his every move. A quick check around proved it was only his teeth chattering. Now he began to be afraid. In the sleeping workshop, all the unfinished and newly finished noises lay silent. Mister Bing stepped cautiously among the workbenches, his ear cocked. Suddenly, CREEEEeeeeeeK! Again!

Mister Bing spun around quickly and struck out wildly in the dark — a hard blow with the ZWIPPP. The ZWIPPP gave a mighty **KLONGGGGG**, followed by a weird **PFLUMMMPF**, as the shadowy figure tumbled to the floor.

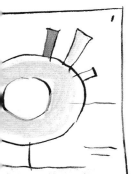

Mister Bing rushed to turn on the light. The intruder was not a pretty sight; wielded blindly, the *ZWIPPP* had made a dreadful lump on his skull. Moreover – and quite curiously – the *ZWIPPP*, badly damaged by the blow, no longer sounded as it once had, but now insisted upon going ZlooouOOooup.

When the mysterious visitor came to, Mister Bing handed him over to the police who questioned him sternly. Frightened, exhausted, dispirited, he admitted that he had been behind the defective *SkoOOBOOoom* and (without any prodding) that he had filched the precious *TrooLOOOOlooo*. That was why he'd come back: to swipe something that would be easier to copy, because he wasn't able to master the intricate mechanism of the *TrooLOOOOlooo*. Then he just broke down in tears.

To keep swindlers from starting competing businesses, Mister Bing made a decision: from now on, each and every product he invented and manufactured would bear his trademark. And just so his customers could be sure of the difference between noises marked "Bing" and worthless knock-offs, he would start an advertising campaign. It was he, alone, who came up with that unforgettable slogan.

Not long afterward — and just so matters would be clear — he displayed a selection of his inventions for the public.

Outstanding! You are a true artist.
I'm a big fan of your *Schwumps*.
As for your *Pruttka*, I spoke of it
yesterday to a friend of mine, a
collector. . . . Your work is an
unimaginable reconciliation of
visual vibration and sonic space.
You absolutely must — if you are
in agreement — allow me to
organize an exhibition in Japan!

I don't like it!

Yecch!

You like them?
I have plenty more
back at my workshop.

It's funny . . . it's silly.

And so the years rolled by. One day, Mister Bing Junior took over, and the little firm grew into an industrial giant. Young Jean-Louis pursued a single goal: to flood the market. With this thought in mind, he set out to mass-produce his father's inventions, the ones that had been the toast of all Tokyo.

Nowadays, Mister Bing Junior, ever the efficient executive, amasses plenty of successes but also a few criticisms. Admirers from the old days have gone so far as to claim that the latest creation from the Bing workshops – for example the discreet **BLOOPEEEE** – would never found a place in the catalogue in the good old days.

As for Mister Bing Senior, he departed
this world some time ago for a realm of
infinite silence . . . where, frankly, he is
really *very* bored.

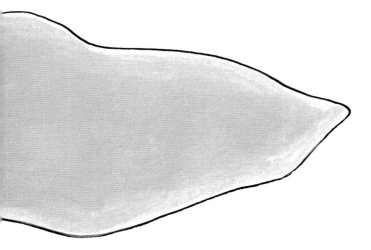

First published in the United States by
DAVID R. GODINE · *Publisher*
Post Office Box 450
Jaffrey, New Hampshire 03452
www.godine.com

Originally published in French as *Le Marchand de bruits*
by Editions Nathan, Paris, France
Copyright © 2002 Editions Nathan/VUEF
Translation copyright © 2006 by Carl W. Scarbrough

LIBRARY OF CONGRESS CATALOGING-IN-PUBLICATION DATA
Rozen, Anna, 1960–
[Marchand de bruits. English]
The merchant of noises / by Anna Rozen ; illustrated by François Avril ;
translated from the French by Carl W. Scarbrough.
p.   cm.
Summary: Inspired by the sound of a twig falling on a dried-out
tree stump in the forest, clever inventor Mr. Bing starts making and
selling noises, which turns into a successful business venture.
ISBN 1-56792-321-6 (hardcover : alk. paper)
[1. Sound—Fiction. 2. Business enterprises—Fiction.]
I. Avril, François, 1961– , ill. II. Scarbrough, Carl W. III. Title.
PZ7 .R8 2Me 2006
[E]—dc22
2006023452

FIRST EDITION
Printed in China